T0113332

SCRATCH PAD

RAMONA SAPPHIRE

authorHOUSE®

AuthorHouse™
1663 Liberty Drive
Bloomington, IN 47403
www.authorhouse.com
Phone: 1 (800) 839-8640

Published by AuthorHouse 09/22/2016

ISBN: 978-1-5246-4133-7 (sc)
ISBN: 978-1-5246-4132-0 (e)

Author's Note

Thanks so much for selecting my publication for your reading pleasure. I enjoy writing stories on assorted topics based on experience and overall -- imagination. I'll admit I'm a bit eccentric and quirky. Many of my stories may comprise an element of inspiration, are outrageous, raunchy, mysterious, bizarre, insightful, or even simple, to say the least.

A very special thanks to those who believed in me, inspired, pushed, and supported me, and appreciated my own distinct style of story-telling rather comparing me to others.

Very special thanks to the well-meaning critics that compelled the necessary *expedient* changes. Your expertise has been far-reaching and helpful, for which I am eternally grateful.

Foremost, are my thanks to God via the gift of breath and hence the wit, imagination, strength, and courage to inspire others and to keep dreaming and pushing.

Prologue

UNKNOWN: *"Just last week, lying next to me was a dead woman whose throat I'd just slashed. I was callously lingering in a pool of her blood. Whores are undeserving; they're as worthless as my mother was. She too was a whore who'd bequeath me with twelve bad-ass siblings with different baby daddies. I had to vie for every morsel of affection and attention. She eventually abandoned all of us and I fell into the throes of remorse and depression all alone in that gloomy castle-like orphanage. All the siblings were separated. And it wasn't until recently that I'd come in contact with one of them. He'd found me through the Internet and I'd just arrived in London a week ago to reunite with him. Consequently, it is a stretch for me to share anything—particularly my heart. I laid there beside this young creature of about twenty-five years my junior, examining the gash in her throat I'd so skillfully crafted like a surgeon. I'd slashed it slowly and deeply as she yelped for mercy and drew her last breath. The sex was lewd and brutal; I'd taken my sweet time. Earlier I'd punched her in her face, disfiguring her gravely. She howled in agony and terror. When she attempted to escape, I snatched her by her amber-streaked tresses as she squirmed and resisted me. An ample tract of weave dislodged from her scalp. Incensed, I tossed her roughly on the bed and* *proceeded to brutalize her as she begged for mercy that merely fell on my deaf deranged ears. She was mine--all mine as I diminished her to an empty shell of herself. I was determined to avenge my mother through my victim's tortured soul."*

Chapter One

"Ah!" screamed Virginia to high heaven when she spotted her svelte, faux-fur-trimmed poncho-wearing sister. It'd been years since they'd hung out. She eyed her admiringly and said, "Looking jazzy as usual, sis."

"Thanks, sis. You look mavalous yourself."

Virginia popped from her seat in the baggage claim area when she saw Georgia approaching. They shared a tight hug and bevy of *"Ah!"*, *"Hey girl!"*, and *"I'm so happy to see you!"*

Virginia was a rather bubbly attractive young woman sporting fashionable jeans, a snug sweater, hip-length jacket, and pointy toed shoes. She lunged for Georgia's luggage who said, "Oh, no, that's heavy, I'll take it."

"No, I got this, sis. You're my guest and I wanna be a good hostess."

"Oh-kaaay! I'mma let you do your thing, girl." And the two strolled through the exit to the parking lot.

Meanwhile, cradled in the seat was the little scratch pad Virginia had been compiling notes in for weeks. In her excitement she'd forgotten about it.

Two weeks ago, Virginia decided she needed to mastermind a winner this time or risk truly being a washout. She perceived her friends clowning her behind her back.

"I told you she sucked. All that wasted effort and money she sank into those piddly stories trying to be a wannabe writer. What a shame."

Virginia set out to prove them wrong and hence devised a plot—one so absurd that no one would believe *she* came up with it. She spent umpteen nights burning the midnight oil, guzzling pots of coffee, and carefully devising the outline— the beginning, middle, and end.

Virginia had already created a name and proceeded to match her storyline to it. She judged her ideas to be farfetched. Regardless, she'd employ them anyway and fine-tune them as she proceeded or stuff evolved in her head.

Everything needed to be cohesive and flow. She'd set a deadline for completion. And then everything got screwed up after leaving the little scratch pad on the seat at the LaGuardia airport in New York.

Dammit to hell!

Chapter Two

"This is a neat little scratch pad," muttered Winston, lifting it from the seat in the luggage claim section of New York's LaGuardia Airport. "Hmm, somebody seemed to be scribbling some juicy stuff in here."

Winston, somewhat effeminate, slender, and sharply dressed, stared at the notes in the little scratch pad and quipped, hmm, what a neat idea, and stuffed it in his back pocket. The little scratch pad contained several pages with less than a quarter of it completed.

Winston seized his bag, headed for the exit, and flagged a cab. Traveling along, he scribbled a few notes in the little scratch pad attempting to complete some of the thoughts therein.

It was a balmy evening. The cab driver experienced a bit of frustration attempting to weave through the thick traffic. Pedestrians flooded the streets and walkways like ants reminiscent of Grand Central Station.

The cab finally arrived at its destination and Winston tipped the cab driver who sighed in relief. The driver headed to the back to fetch the luggage from his trunk as Winston was returning the change from his fare to his wallet. He lunged for the door and the little scratch pad tumbled out his back pocket unwittingly. He retrieved his luggage from the driver, tipped his head, and headed into his apartment.

The cab driver tarried along and retrieved another passenger. He placed the luggage in the trunk and held the door open for his passenger, closed it afterwards, and dove into the driver's seat.

This time it was a middle-aged woman, who was rather petite. Keeping trim and fit was her personal philosophy on youthfulness. She appeared disheveled about something as the driver observed her boo-hooing in the back seat even before he pulled off.

As compassionately as possible the driver whispered, "Where to ma'am?"

"I don't know; anywhere."

"I'm sorry you're upset ma'am, but I have to take you somewhere, otherwise you'll simply be paying for us to sit here with the meter running."

The woman abruptly balled into her hanky and the driver sympathized and decided to shut off the meter. Besides, the previous rider had awarded him with a rather fat tip.

"Okay, I'm ready," said the passenger, blowing her nose and releasing her last whimper and sniffle. "Take me to the airport. I'm off to the UK. Someone awaits me there I should've married in the first damn place!"

"Alrighty then," said the driver not wishing to pry or get involved for that matter. "I'm off."

The passenger whose name was Charlotte, noticed the little scratch pad wedged between the door and the back seat. She eyed it curiously and cracked it open.

Charlotte read the contents of the little scratch pad with a bit of excitement in her eyes. She decided to join the bandwagon and jot in it herself.

"What ch'ou got there?" asked the driver. "You seem ecstatic by the expression on your face," he said, eyeing her in the rear-view mirror.

"A little scratch pad someone left behind with some interesting notes inside."

"Oh, the passenger before you must've dropped it. You can hand it to me and I can…"

"Not on your life, buster!" said Charlotte. "Finders--keepers, losers--weepers. It's mine now. Besides I need it to draft a letter I want to send to my no-good husband. He's going to be shocked to find me gone when he returns home from work!" she snickered.

"Well, if you don't mind my asking, and I don't usually like to pry, won't he be worried sick?"

"And?"

"Gotcha," said the driver. And he backed off and focused more intensely on the road and his destination.

Benny, the cabby, eyed the skyline and the cityscape admiringly. It was dusk and the sky was a breathtaking turquoise-orange-blue. There was a subtle breeze flowing through his slightly cracked window. He was relieved he no longer needed the air conditioning that'd earlier siphoned much of his gas.

Benny arrived at the airport and pulled up to the curbside for the airline departing to London. Charlotte tipped the driver and awaited her luggage from the trunk.

Charlotte rolled her suitcase to the ticket counter whereupon she was requested to present her passport. She released the handle of her suitcase and set it on the scale.

Charlotte was carting a shoulder bag and she opened it to retrieve her passport. However, it didn't seem apparent on sight.

Charlotte worried some, certain she'd retrieved it from the dresser. She dumped her purse and riffled through her things until she eyed it.

"Whew! That was close!" she muttered to the desk attendant. And she proceeded to return everything to her purse. Somehow in the process the little scratch pad made a beeline for the floor unbeknownst to her. And after her bags were checked and whisked away, she proceeded to the security baggage check and her flight gate.

Chapter Three

Chandler stood behind Charlotte at the ticket counter and nearly kicked the little scratch pad as it was his turn. He bent over and retrieved it.

"What's this?" he muttered to himself, and shoved it in his jacket pocket.

Chandler, a rather short chunky fella with a noticeable gut, in his mid-forties, and in a business suit, completed his transaction and headed to the security baggage check area. While standing in the line all the way to the wazoo, he remembered the little scratch pad tucked away in his pocket with a couple of pens.

He pulled out his pens and the little scratch pad and began skimming it. Hmm, interesting little stuff in here, I must say, he quipped. I'mma jot some stuff down in it too. Let's see here...

Chandler shortly stepped up to the line, removed his shoes, and placed everything into containers, including the little scratch pad and pens. After being probed and scanned and tagged all clear, he retrieved his containers from the conveyer belt and proceeded to don his shoes.

Chandler headed to his flight gate unaware he'd left one more basket behind with the little scratch pad and pens he'd had in his pocket. He continued on his merry way none the wiser.

"You left a basket behind, sir!" yelled the security attendant. Chandler was long gone down the escalator out of earshot.

The attendant, Alford, a rather chunky, graying, apple-shaped, middle-aged man, examined the contents of the basket and muttered, "This just looks like some junk except…. what have we here?"

Alford lifted the little scratch pad from the basket and proceeded to peer inside. He gapped his eyes upon peeping the contents and covertly stuffed it in his back pocket.

"This is some good stuff in here," Alford said later, reading it during his coffee break. "Hmm, it looks like several penmanship styles in here. I think I'mma join the bandwagon too," he muttered.

Alford became so engrossed in his writing the time escaped him. His supervisor, Madison, rushed over and said gruffly, "You were supposed to relieve me ten minutes ago!"

"Oh, I'm sorry!" said Alford. And he jetted, seizing his cell phone, glasses, and newspaper, inadvertently leaving the little scratch pad on the table. It'd slid out his newspaper when he'd stuffed it in there attempting to hide it from his boss.

Madison, a tall, middle-aged man of girth, with a mustache, sat in Alford's seat and opened the little scratch pad. He was caught up momentarily and scribbled something in it. Next, he headed over to a coffee vendor and ordered a fresh cup of coffee. He momentarily laid the little scratch pad on the counter to reach for his wallet.

Madison paid for the coffee and returned to his table. He was about to pull the scratch pad out and realized he'd left it on the counter. He scurried back to the vendor but the little scratch pad was gone!

"Oh, snap!" he muttered to himself.

Chapter Four

An Asian woman named Lola, frail and petite, but rather stylish, was next in line for her coffee. She scoped the little scratch pad lying on the counter. She glanced around for the patron who was in front of her and didn't spot him. She ordered a bottle of green tea and stashed it and the little scratch pad in her large over-stuffed shopping bag and headed for her boarding gate.

Lola selected a seat and made herself comfy. After about ten minutes, she managed to pull out the little scratch pad and began reading. She was awestruck by the contents. She experienced a gamut of emotions as she read, from snickering, to whimpering, to balking, and silence. It was the most intriguing little scratch pad to her.

Lola too noticed the varied penmanship styles inside and decided to take a stab at writing in the little scratch pad. She began to scribble memoirs of her days in Korea during and after the war.

Buckets of tears streamed from Lola's eyes as she finished scribbling. Her gate was called and she hurried and gathered her things and boarding ticket and stuffed the little scratch pad in her bag.

Lola arrived in her seat and made herself comfy. It would be a long flight to Korea. During her flight, she acquired some shut-eye, gazed at movies, enjoyed meals, and cocktails.

Lola finally reached her destination and unboarded her flight. She was anxious to see loved ones she'd left behind during her stent in America.

Lola headed for the luggage claim section to retrieve her bags. Her Aunt was waiting for her who approached her and hugged her tightly. They began conversing in their native tongue. During the process, somehow the little scratch pad escaped from Lola's over-stuffed bag. Her uncle, who'd just arrived from parking, hugged her and seized her luggage. They all headed for the parking lot.

Chapter Five

The little scratch pad was inadvertently kicked across the floor. It landed against the heel of Alec, a tall, handsome, thirtyish, athletic-looking man in khaki shorts and a Dashiki. He reached down and snagged it and muttered, "What's this?" with a thick African accent, and shoved it into his Dashiki pocket.

Alec's destination was South Africa. He'd just wrapped up a conference and was heading toward the ticket counter and then onto security baggage check. He'd made a pit stop over the weekend before the conference.

After being cleared, Alec scurried to his gate and boarded a flight to South Africa. The flight was relatively unremarkable and he unboarded and headed to baggage claim.

When Alec arrived, the carousel was empty of luggage and the area filled with antsy passengers. Miraculously, he found a seat and sat with his head tilted back and his eyelids were heavy as lead. He nodded off a bit and his head rocked backward and jerked forward. This startled him and he suddenly remembered the little scratch pad in his Dashiki pocket.

Alec opened the little scratch pad and his eyes popped. He was amazed at the contents. He too underwent a gamut of emotions and elected to add to it. He scribbled something briefly and just like that, the luggage began shuffling through the portal and onto the carousel.

Alec recognized his luggage instantly attributed to Sapphire with Passion's dazzling luggage jewels, exited the airport, and hailed a cab. He was homeward bound wherein his wife was waiting anxiously to hear the details of his journey.

The sky was a spectacular orange-red-golden-turquoise-purple backdrop traveling the coastal roads of Cape Town. Witnessed were the amazing vistas, incredible mountains and boulders, and the spectacular Atlantic Ocean.

The cab driver hopped out the cab and retrieved his passenger's luggage from the trunk. Alec accepted the luggage and tipped the driver. As he was fumbling with his wallet, the little scratch pad fell out his pocket.

The cabby, Gulliver, waived farewell to his passenger and was about to close the back passenger door when the little scratch pad became wedged therein. He reached down to fetch the little scratch pad and tried to hail Alec who was long gone and disappeared into his magnificent villa.

"Oh well," muttered Gulliver to himself. "It's just a little ole scratch pad." And he tossed it in the glove compartment.

Gulliver returned his cab to the cab garage late that night and it was off to home and bed he went. He'd entirely forgotten about the little scratch pad.

Chapter Six

Fran selected her cab from the cab garage and headed to Durbanville to retrieve her American passenger to take him to the airport. He was headed for the UK then onto America.

Fran threw his bag into the trunk and held the door open for him. That is one fine hunk of a man, she quipped.

Throughout the entire drive to the airport she peeped him through the rearview mirror. The last time he threw her for a loop when he caught her red-handed and stared back.

Abruptly the passenger informed Fran he needed to stop at a toilet before he arrived at the airport. The traffic was too thick and he knew he couldn't contain himself until then.

Fran smiled at him and said, "You're not about to ditch me are you?"

"Oh no, my luggage is here--remember? I really have to pee now. I'll be right back."

The passenger, whose name was Magellan, was a dark-complexioned man, thirty something, quite handsome, cut, and a wannabe-thug, hip-hop artist with dreads. He hopped out the vehicle and fled to the restroom. Fran waited for about thirty seconds before she remembered she'd opened the glove compartment earlier to stash her today's mail into it for perusal later. And there was the little scratch pad seemingly awaiting patiently for new eyes to open it.

"What's this?" muttered Fran. And she opened it and gasped in surprise. She actually hoped Magellan would take a little while longer to enable her to read the amazing contents. Besides, the meter was running and big dollars were about to flow her way.

Fran took the time to scribble some stuff in the little scratch pad and kept waiting for her passenger to return. She wasn't worried; only ten minutes had passed. And just as she got to the juiciest parts, Magellan abruptly arrived, knocking on the window smiling, exposing pearly even teeth.

Fran unlocked the door for him and permitted him entry. "I'm not holding you up, am I?" questioned Magellan.

"No sweat," Fran responded. Really? she quipped. The meter had been running the entire time Magellan was gone unbeknownst to him. Ka-ching!

They arrived at the airport and Fran showed Magellan the little scratch pad. "Is this yours?" she asked flirtatiously. "I found it in the cab," she fibbed.

After perusing a few pages, Magellan responded half-heartedly, "Yes, that's mine. Thank you for finding it for me."

Fran chuckled at his deception and headed to the back of the cab and pulled her passenger's luggage from the trunk. Magellan stared at the meter and gasped. He pulled out his wallet and paid Fran as she rolled up with his luggage.

Magellan had slipped the little scratch pad into his back pocket by then. He couldn't wait to examine the contents further and eke out something.

Magellan arrived in London and hailed a taxi to his hotel. The inside was plush with high-end classical British velvety furnishings and adornments.

He settled in, had high tea, and retired to his suite to catch a little TV. Abruptly he remembered the little scratch pad and pulled it out to examine it. He was amused by all the stuff inside, especially something in particular. He scribbled in the pad and chuckled.

Magellan was in London to meet up with friends and family and on other business, one of which would be retrieving him from the hotel soon. He'd insisted on coming to the hotel first to have some me-time and relaxation.

At some point, Magellan impetuously changed his plans and called his friend, Parker, to request he wait another few days before retrieving him, to which he agreed. Two days later Magellan scribbled again in the little scratch pad and afterwards laid it on the night stand along with the phone and another scratch pad and pencil.

When it was finally time to leave, Magellan reached for the little scratch pad, however got it crossed with the hotel one instead. He was none the wiser.

Chapter Seven

Later on that afternoon, the housekeeper, Valencia, a rather, short, attractive, child-bearing-aged, Hispanic woman, arrived to change the bedding and discovered the little scratch pad on the table. She knew the room wouldn't be occupied for a while and she decided to sneak a smoke break and read the contents.

Her eyes bucked and she was enchanted for some time. She became so engrossed in the contents and scribbling notes inside, she didn't hear her supervisor come in 'till it was too late.

The supervisor tapped Valencia on the shoulder and asked, "What are you doing?" scaring the bejezus out of her. Valencia inadvertently dropped the little scratch pad that fell beside the bed.

"I'm sorry boss. Please don't write me up. I can guarantee it won't happen again."

Valencia had three stair-step kids, five, seven, and nine. Thus her supervisor empathized with her being a single mom herself. "Okay, but don't let it happen again. The other supervisor is not going to be as lenient with you as I if she catches you."

"Don't worry, she won't," said Valencia. And in her haste to finish cleaning, she'd forgotten the fallen little scratch pad and scurried to the next room.

Later on that evening the next occupant arrived. Hudson was a fortyish, sharply dressed, successful man with a whole lot of swag. He was rather tired from the long drive and ready to retire to bed even though it was quite early, eight o'clock. He decided to order a cocktail and a snack and called for room service.

Room Service arrived not long after that and Hudson partook of the cocktail and snack and eventually crashed. Earlier, he'd jumped out of bed and reached for his slippers before heading for the restroom. As he felt for them, he inadvertently uncovered the little scratch pad.

"What's this?" Hudson muttered. And he pried it open. Upon reviewing the last entry, he remarked, "Yikes! This one would've been foolish to expose *himself* after writing *this* stuff. That was smart of him to remain anonymous—not that everyone else used their real names for that matter," he chuckled aloud.

Next he discovered something remarkable evidently everyone else had missed. He acknowledged it and made an advantageous decision. He closed his eyes and crashed.

Hudson arrived at the LaGuardia Airport the next day. He was on a mission besides heading for home, tired than a mofo. He made a pit stop after he claimed his luggage at the baggage claim and proceeded through the exit to the car that awaited him outside.

Chapter Eight

Meanwhile, back home, Virginia had mourned the loss of her little scratch pad over the past few weeks. It was her pride and joy and the best storyline she could muster for the time being. She would have enjoyed her sister's visit more thoroughly had she not been preoccupied and agonizing over her little scratch pad. It was her saving grace and light at the end of her tunnel of writer's block. And she perceived she would've no longer been the laughing stock of her friends.

It was a warm sunny day in Manhattan and traffic was thicker than a mug. Nevertheless, Virginia and her sister, Georgia, managed to make it to the airport in ample time. Upon arrival, they exchanged tight hugs, kisses, and tears, and Georgia headed up the escalator to the ticket counter.

It'd never occurred to Virginia to check the Lost and Found to see if anyone had turned in her little scratch pad. She'd reasoned, why would they? It was miniscule with illegible scribbling and muddled thoughts. She was certain it was tossed, so she imagined.

And just as Virginia was making a beeline for the exit, a call came through on her cell phone.

"Are you Virginia?" the caller asked.

"Yes, who's calling?" she asked, noting the strange number on the caller I.D. Normally she didn't respond to such calls, however, she had a hunch and obeyed it.

"Hudson," he responded. "I found your little scratch pad beside my hotel bed all the way in London. I just happened to notice your name and phone number scribbled on the back inside cover. It's at the Lost and Found section of the LaGuardia Airport."

Virginia was ecstatic! She couldn't believe her ears! She was doing the '*Carlton*' dance in her mind."

"Oh my God! I've been looking for that for two weeks! Thank You! Thank you! Thank you!"

"Heah, before I hang up, Virginia, I'd like to say just one thing to you that I hope will inspire you to finish your writing project."

"What's that, Hudson?"

"You are one helluva writer and you should definitely finish your project and get it published. Perhaps you can revise your original storyline and incorporate the contents of the scratch pad. You'll see what I mean when you retrieve it. In fact, I can give you the number of a damn good publisher friend of mine who will ensure your book is not only published, but slated for the New York Times Bestseller List. I got goose bumps reading it. I can text you his number and info."

"Oh my God! You just don't know what this means to me. None of my friends have faith in my ability and this will blow the roof off of things!"

"Well good luck, Virginia. And do I have your word you will follow through? Perhaps after you receive the text we can meet privately and discuss your future?"

"Sure, most definitely, Hudson!"

"Well, as soon as we hang up, I will text you the info!"

"Thank you, Hudson!"

Shortly after the call ended, Hudson texted the information as promised. Virginia promptly added him as a new contact in her phone.

Virginia rushed to retrieve her little scratch pad and was amazed at all the stories therein. It was quite overwhelming and some of the penmanship was nearly illegible. However, she managed to make out the words or adlib.

Virginia decided to size up each character, tweaking as necessary to make the stories pop. There were poems, letters, musings, and such. She would try to include them all.

Chapter Nine

WINSTON: He was a yuppie Renaissance man impeccably dressed. He wrote:

"I arrived at the funeral and immediately spotted you, my ex. I wanted to choke your ass! There you stood tall and sexy as ever on the arm of my former best friend who purported to be straight. All along, he was perpetrating a fraud and planned to seduce you from the get go. I only came because your dad was like a father to me. As I stood over his coffin weeping, I ashamedly wished it was you lying there. Your dad was one of the coolest and least judgmental straight people I'd ever met. In fact, he said he loved me unconditionally like his own flesh and blood. And he shared with me that he was angered you had chosen 'that trifling, gold digging, creep,' over me. It was no doubt awkward and emotional being in your presence. Nevertheless, I needed to come to honor your dad. And though I miss your town, our conversations, and the life we shared, despite my feelings, I have moved on. I have an extraordinary loving and giving partner awaiting me back home. Any day now, we will be parents. May you both rot in hell!!!!"

CHARLOTTE: She was a proclaimed cougar who was twelve years her husband's senior. The corners of her eyes were garnished with crow's feet. She was insecure about her age and required validation by younger men.

"*When I arrived home early from work yesterday, you didn't see or hear me come in. I'd changed into a sexy nightie downstairs purchased along the way that was meticulously selected. I crept up the stairs all hot and bothered and heard sex noises. I gingerly approached the door of our bedroom and there you were buried deep between your sister's thighs. Imagine my horror, shame, and rage! At this point, I ceased to be incognito and screamed your name, and as you know, you heard me. Next I fled downstairs and out the door like a bat out of hell. Later I returned to pack my bags when I knew you'd be gone and read the note you left me. All this time, you'd been screwing your so-called 'baby sister', Savannah. Because your parents died, I had not an inkling or recourse to doubt your claim. So all these years you've been flaunting Savannah as your sister while cheating right under my nose. I thought I detected bizarre nuances between you two here and there. However, I chose to ignore my hunches. Besides, it wouldn't have dawned on me to check her out. After all, she was rather endearing and accommodating. Really? This is unacceptable and I've left your sorry ass for good! Good luck with your 'sister' and good riddance!!!*"

CHANDLER: He was a clean-cut conservative middle-aged life coach with an abrasive controlling bitter aunt. She was his sole provider who reared him after his parents were killed in a hit-and-run vehicle accident as a child. His resentment of her was deeply embedded in his consciousness. He must've scribbled ***"I HATE YOU!"*** a hundred times in the scratch pad. Chandler often harped on a childhood memory. His aunt would chastise him when he misbehaved, being his typical pubescent self, by making him sit at a table, hours on end, writing repetitive demeaning things about himself such as 'I am a bad boy,' 'I will be good.' Perhaps this was a reflection of her frustration of being a spinster and losing her only living blood relative. She was unaware of the emasculating effect she had upon him.

Returning home from his conference, Chandler pushed through his front door. He waded through a sea of electronic gadgets and a hodge-podge of wires, cords, papers, refuse, clothing, magazines, and other stuff cluttering his apartment.

He immediately shed his attire, including a pair of fire engine red lacy panties, and showered. Lastly, he indulged in a snack and attempted to crash.

Fired up from his conference and traumatized from visiting his ailing aunt, Chandler recited his usual mantra when he had insomnia, ***"I HATE YOU!!!"*** repeatedly until he crashed.

ALFORD: He disguised his handwriting paranoid he'd be identified. After all, what if he inadvertently laid the scratch pad around? He'd just come from the doctor's office yesterday with a dirty bill of health. Recently he'd felt drained and woozy and had an urgent need to urinate throughout the day. He'd observed his unexplained weight loss. And after a thorough examination with his physician, he was diagnosed with diabetes mellitus type 2. This required him to eat more frequently, at least every three hours, up from every four to six hours. Alford wrote:

"How in the hell am I gonna explain my health condition to my supervisor? I'm skating on thin ice approaching retirement age as it is. This constant peeing is getting out of hand. What

in the hell am I gonna do? I'm beginning to look like an owl staying up nights worrying about this."

MADISON: He'd taken Alford's spot at the table. Upon reviewing his musings, resentments about his son surfaced. He was a slouch and a moocher who was constantly babied by his mother. He never seemed to be able to hold down a job or a residence. Madison was frustrated by his wife's constant interference with his raising of their son. She'd turned him into a wuss to him. However, he was hopeful having his son work with him would be a blessing; that he'd become more responsible under his supervision and finally man up and get a place of his own. He wrote:

"So what's this Alford wrote? I'm assuming this is Alford's entry since it's the last one. Oh my; so that's why he takes so many breaks. Do you think I give a damn? My son needs a job! I'mma turn his ass in!"

LOLA: Reflecting on her memoirs, Lola relayed:

"Back at home during the Korean war, I and my fiancé, Harlow, were very much in love. I waited for years for his return from the war, expecting to get married right away. Living in abject poverty and being yet unmarried, I was unable to contribute to my household. My family was expecting me to marry any day now; however, I'd received word Harlow was killed in the war. I kept this from my parents fearing I'd be tossed in the street. Even so, I elected to leave anyway so as not to be a burden and resorted to prostitution to survive. I began writing my memoirs stating how I would stay away from home for days, cavorting with different lovers. Most of them were American soldiers who treated me like the slut I was

portraying. Eventually I'd become strung out on heroin but managed to beat it cold turkey following umpteen attempts. After being beaten several times and winding up left for dead in a ditch, I'd managed to pull myself out and wound up in a woman's shelter. I perceived my family had assumed I'd gotten married and moved on. At the time I was on the other side of the country and had no means of looking them up. Eventually, being petite, I'd managed to stow away on a cargo ship heading to America. I'd hidden in a large laundry duffle bag from a Korean dry cleaning merchant I'd become employed with after becoming clean. Upon my arrival in America, I found myself destitute and hooking again to make ends meet. I didn't know the language at first, but managed to learn by watching cartoons. Later I met and married Austin, who owned a dry cleaner and recently died, only two years ago. Sadly, we never had children. I guess I'd gotten punched once too many. He stayed with me anyway. You gotta love him for that. Clearly he was in it for the long haul. Now it's time for me to return home to reconnect with my family. They're all I have left. I'm ecstatic about seeing them. Thank God for the Internet!"

ALEC: He was a happily-married African gynecologist. However, there was one catch-- though he loved his wife, Mika dearly, he secretly despised children. Nevertheless, it was African tradition to have heirs, which he abided by. He was rather superficial and judged a baby would disrupt his home life and destroy Mika's looks.

Mika was gorgeous and slim and mindful of her figure. Alec had enlisted a second and third wife to sire two children apiece that would suffice as heirs. Most of their time was consumed tending to them. They each lived in separate dwellings on the villa property. This freed him up to pamper his favorite wife whom he desired all to himself.

Mika was resentful of Alec's other wives and desperately wanted a child of her own. She'd observe her husband's wives tending to their children and wish she could be a mother too. She constantly whined to Alec about this to his chagrin. She and Alec had tried numerous times, so she imagined, but to no avail. She'd seen a physician who'd reported she was fine. Unbeknownst to Mika, Alec would crush up birth-control pills and slip them into her beverage. This finally played out for him and he'd made a decision. Alec wrote:

"My vasectomy was successful. At last my darling, I'll have you all to myself for certain. You will never be the wiser."

FRAN: She had an upbeat personality and appeared somewhat eccentric gathered by her musings about her passenger. She wrote:

"I have a crush on you as you may already know from us playing eye tag in the rearview mirror. While you were in the restroom, I discovered this quirky little scratch pad with all sorts of cool and juicy stuff inside. I don't know if you like wiry blue-eyed White girls, but I thought I'd take a chance and a stab at writing you a poem. It's about my passion for 'coffee' and the effect it has on me; and it goes like this:

'MIDNIGHT BREW'

"You excite my thirst with your mellow aroma.
I crave your steamy hot essence at bizarre
hours of each day and night.
Yet I savor you only by day. For at nightfall you
leave me thrashing in wide-eyed frenzy.
When I partake of you, every sip invigorates
my taste buds to ecstasy.
*With ever swig of you **I savor** your pure black freshness.*
I cling to you for energy enthusiasm and enlightenment.
I binge on you with thirsting passion and devotion.
The stroke of you with my lips and tongue turns me out.
And without you I'm groggy, sluggish, devastated,
all of which arouses my thirst again.
So I quench my thirst with your rich black substance
again, and again, and again 'till I've reached my peak.
But then I crash. The bitterness has swelled in my mouth.
Intimidated, you're no longer fresh and responsive to me.
Gradually I've discovered I've guzzled too much.
Now I'm overwhelmed and delusional and
frantic to get you out of my system.
And no sooner than I do, the emptiness becomes too
unbearable so I scramble desperately for another refill!

And that's that piece and I hope you like it. So okay, here's another one..." Ooops, here he comes! quipped Fran.

MAGELLAN: He assumed Fran concealed the pad and then passed it onto him gathered by his response:

"She must think I'm slow, trying to fake me out like she's talkin' about coffee. I know she recognized me and the gold-digger was even tryin' to pass me her digits. I'm sorry but I just don't do White girls. No offense, but I happen to love my sisters with their juicy butts and lips. And one more thing..."

Magellan must've gotten interrupted by a phone call because he didn't complete his sentence. Following a soft knock, Magellan opened his hotel room door after vaguely recognizing the voice on the other side. His eyes popped when he stared into the face of his former lover, Charlotte, at least fifteen years his senior. She leaped into his arms instantaneously and the pair clawed and slobbered each other down.

For the unscrupulous, there was nothing like the heat between a cougar and a young buck. And after their sordid lovemaking over the next few days, Magellan scribbled in the scratch pad whilst starring into the face of Charlotte curled up in blissful slumber:

"For me the lust is still there but the love is gone in my heart. I need to be real with Charlotte and tell her how I feel; that she's just too old for me now and I'm no longer attracted. I feel sorry for her but she's got to bounce tonight. I'm meeting my fiancé tomorrow and have a show to do. Charlotte appears a tad frustrated and I don't care to be her channel of release even if the sex is juicy. But I've got to find the right way to relay it to keep her from snappin', my being a celebrity and all."

VALENCIA: She was a good mother to her children though she had a weakness for men that prompted her to be attracted for all the wrong reasons to her demise. She wrote:

*"My children are my pride and joy, but God knows sometimes I curse the day they were born. I try my damnedest, which never seems to be enough. I'm ashamed of how I'm feeling right now, but I'm only being honest with myself. Every woman dreams of the Big D. But let me tell you, if you've never had it, it ain't all it's cracked up to be. Contrary to belief, I'm old-fashioned. I believe the dog should chase the cat. But next thing you know you're the one chasing the dog, and your tail's between **your** legs. Next, your heart's possessed, you're whipped like mashed potatoes, your head's spinning, your snatch is throbbin', and slam, bam, thank you, ma'am, BULLYA! Three kids and three baby daddies! I'm venting now, but after a long hard day's work, nothing brings me more joy than seeing my babies after all. Thank God I'm blessed with a supervisor who's practically in the same boat as I, barring a few dollars. Uh oh, here she comes now!"*

Earlier Valencia's supervisor was banging the well-endowed maintenance man in the broom closet while she was stuck with all the suites to clean alone.

UNKNOWN: *"Just last week, lying next to me was a dead woman whose throat I'd just slashed. I was callously lingering in a pool of her blood. Whores are undeserving; they're as worthless as my mother was. She too was a whore who'd bequeath me with twelve bad-ass siblings with different baby daddies. I had to vie for every morsel of affection and attention. She eventually abandoned all of us and I fell into the throes of remorse and depression all alone in that gloomy castle-like* orphanage. All the siblings were separated. And it wasn't until recently that I'd come in contact with one of them. He found me through the Internet and I'd just arrived in London a week ago to reunite with him. Consequently, it is a stretch for me to share anything—particularly my heart. I laid there beside this young creature of about twenty-five years my junior, examining the gash in her throat I'd so skillfully crafted like a surgeon. I'd slashed it slowly and deeply as she yelped for mercy and drew her last breath. The sex was lewd and brutal; I'd taken my sweet time. Earlier I'd punched her in her face, disfiguring her gravely. She howled in agony and terror. When she attempted to escape, I snatched her by her amber-streaked tresses as she squirmed and resisted me. An ample tract of weave dislodged from her scalp. Incensed, I tossed her roughly on the bed and proceeded to brutalize her as she begged for mercy that merely fell on my deaf deranged ears. She was mine--all mine as I diminished her to an empty shell of herself. I was determined to avenge my mother through my victim's tortured soul."

Chapter Ten

Virginia and Georgia sat side by side in the reserved row of the packed auditorium. They were squirming and profiling in their seats like rock stars. The lights were low and the audience sounded like a million humming bees.

"Scribble-Mongers' did not make it to the New York Times Bestseller List, however tonight Virginia was being celebrated by a high-profile community organization. She'd not only grown to new heights as a short-story writer, but also become an exemplary community icon.

After wrestling with the idea for a while, Virginia brainstormed with her sister and decided to run a full-scale publishing company. She'd partnered with Georgia, who had a degree in communications, and would serve as editor. Furthermore, she'd reached out to her outstanding fellow artist friend overseas who'd assisted with designing covers and media promotions.

Feeling stripped of moral support by her friends and family, Virginia was leery of support and companionship altogether. However, through prayer and introspection, she realized she was sabotaging her own destiny.

Virginia squashed her fears and reservations with courage and assertively garnered the support she needed.

And after all this positive self-talk and encouragement, through the Creator's grace and goodness, she'd succeeded.

Virginia acknowledging collaboration is key, moved on to newer circles and hosted workshops on self-publishing for adults as well as teens and yes--children. She'd prompted them to sell on-line as well as direct sales as instructed. She'd collaborated with other publishers and such.

Virginia had enlisted all her transcribing coworkers to type the manuscripts of which most were skeptical but a few agreed. And there were oodles and oodles of videos flooded into the market.

So imagine Virginia's excitement at this moment styling in a floor-length black lace gown, black strappy sandals, faux fur shrug, wavy twenties hair-do, and lastly, other accouterments such as a feathered fitted hat with veil, beaded vintage handbag, and forearm-length gloves. The theme for the evening was *'Vintage Moments.'*

Both sisters were impeccably made up and wore bright red glimmering lipstick. And all her team and new close friends and supporters were there for her.

The reception preceding the gala occurred in a large podium-filled hall with decorative tables and several open bars strategically placed throughout. The tables were topped with lavish smorgasbords of finger-foods consisting of veggies, fruit, breads, cheeses, and desserts. The hall buzzed with the lively conversation of the dressed-to-impress attendees. Hudson approached Virginia and congratulated her.

"Why thank you, Hudson, and congratulations to you also on your book making the New York Times Bestsellers List, *Uh-GHIN*, you rascal you. You're a fantastic novelist and media stylist, you know. If it wasn't for you pushing me to finish my book and your excellent videos of my community work, I wouldn't be standing here. I'm forever grateful to you, Hudson," said Virginia, hugging him tightly.

Hudson cast Virginia an endearing smile and strolled over to the appetizers. Virginia noted his swag and eyed him admiringly as he departed.

Currently, Virginia was sipping on Champagne in the auditorium with her head in the clouds, but descended to earth when she heard her name called. She clutched Georgia's hand and they strutted down the isle like two peacocks beaming and profiling to the stage.

"I am grateful and humbled by this honor.... Thank you all for your support and confidence, especially you, Hudson, a warm giving soul and mentor who discovered and believed in me."

Virginia gloated, blowing kisses at Hudson and the packed auditorium. And just before she concluded her speech, she yelled in triumph, "Eat your heart out!" covertly directed at all the Doubting Thomases and naysayers she'd encountered along her journey.

Afterwards, Hudson headed home alone. He was pumped up and wired. He'd squandered nearly his entire book commissions on his lavish lifestyle. There was only one thing left to do.

Chapter Eleven

John approached the counter of the local liquor store and paid the clerk for the whiskey. He was feeling rather energetic and needy and headed outside to his sports vehicle.

It was a warm balmy night in New York. The street lamps glistened. And despite the lateness of the hour, hundreds of New Yorkers scudded about like roaches.

John drove to a shady remote area. He was looking for some action. He paused and guzzled some of the liquor and tossed a bottle out the window. The disorderly shattering of the glass resounded in the distance. He chuckled aloud in a drunken stupor that was intercepted by a disgusting burp.

Briefly, he reflected on his childhood. He envisioned his mother's face in ecstasy surrounded by the sea of men she'd serviced over his lifetime. He balked and sulked in disgust, then recouped with a psychotic sneer.

After sobering up a bit, he drove a brief distance and spotted a wholesome-looking young woman whose name he would learn later was Delta. He lured her into his sports vehicle.

There'd been lately a rash of disappearing strumpets in the area. No one had surfaced to claim them or contest their disappearance.

Residents reported a man in a sports vehicle that would case the area. Mysteriously, they could never identify the vehicle or perpetrator for that matter. He wore shades and darkwear, and the vehicles he drove were never identical. And apparently the license plates were counterfeit…

"Are you the Popo?" asked Delta.

"No, I'm a surgeon, honey. Now how about I take you home and we share a little bubbly and do the nasty?"

"A surgeon, huh? You must be swimming in dough," said Delta, admiringly.

"Pretty much; the sky's the limit. You got any family, honey? Why are you out here like this?"

"Nah, that's why I'm out here; they dissed me. They couldn't care less about me."

"Drugs?"

"No."

"Then what?"

"Look, if you don't mind, I'd rather not talk about it." What shall I call you anyways?" asked John?

"Delta's my name. What about you?"

"John's fine."

"Alrighty then. Pleased to meet you, John."

"Likewise."

John was ecstatic! He'd hit the Jack Pot. She fit his profile to the t!

Delta was aggravated about the third degree. Rehashing her past irked her. No, she wasn't on drugs or pregnant. However, about two years ago, her mother's boyfriend couldn't keep his eyes or hands off her either for that matter. Knowing her mother was weak and vulnerable after an abusive relationship with her father, she decided to simply leave and not stir up any trouble. She judged her mother wouldn't believe her and kick her out in the streets anyway.

Absent the support of love ones and friends, Delta was forced to thrive on the mean streets of Harlem. Eventually, she met a man while pandering who took her in and ultimately turned her out. He'd beat the crap out of her when she'd come up short and accuse her of holding out when in fact, she simply sucked at hooking. Reaching twenty-one a year later was a milestone for her and that's when she decided to book, take her chances, and go for broke...

"Sure, that's okay, honey. Now how about I take you home?" suggested John.

"Huh? Oh, uh where do you live, might I ask?" inquired Delta, recouping and refocusing on John.

"In a swanky penthouse in Manhattan."

"Sure, let's go!" Delta exclaimed, ka-ching-eyed.

Hours later, Delta was naked and sprawled on the bed at a high-end motel in Manhattan. Her throat was slashed and her blood gushing like a waterfall on the fresh towels that were purchased earlier.

John had deceived Delta by foregoing the penthouse, explaining his ailing mother still lived with him; that having company so late would disturb her. The poor unsuspecting slob, so disillusioned by the possibility of a fat paycheck, bought his story.

When they'd arrived at the motel, John had insisted Delta wait in the vehicle while he secured the room. He slipped her inside, back-glancing all along to ensure no one saw them.

Earlier they'd stopped at a nearby twenty four-hour establishment to purchase everything they required, including booze, snacks, and sexy lingerie. However, unbeknownst to Delta, John had an agenda. He'd also made additional purchases of rope, duct tape, switch blades, cleaning agents, travel blankets, and towels, all whilst insisting she wait in his vehicle. He'd meticulously avoided being seen with her.

"Here's to you, mama," toasted John with a slur, raising his Champagne glass, inebriated, and swooning over Delta's body. I'm gonna make you prouda me yet. In fact, I'mma call my next book, *'Make Mama Proud','*" by John Hudson Rivers.

Clearly, Hudson had removed *his* pages before returning the little scratch pad to Virginia. He'd saved it for his current blockbuster novel *'Tortured Soul'* that'd landed him critical acclaim on the New York Times Bestseller List as usual.

Hudson guzzled his Champagne and gloated over his victim. "Good job!" he praised himself aloud with a deranged smile.

The End